This book belongs to:

. . . .

. . . .

Retold by Monica Hughes
Illustrated by Andy Catling

Reading consultants: Betty Root and Monica Hughes

Marks and Spencer p.l.c.
PO Box 3339
Chester, CH99 9QS

shop online
www.marksandspencer.com

ISBN 978-1-84461-856-9
Printed in China

First Readers

The Emperor's New Clothes

MARKS &
SPENCER

Helping your child to read

First Readers are closely linked to the National Curriculum. Their vocabulary has been carefully selected from the word lists recommended by the National Literacy Strategy.

Read the story
Read the story
to your child
a few times.

"The cloth will make beautiful clothes,"
said the tailors.
The emperor loved clothes.
He had rooms full of clothes.
"Make me some new clothes," he said.
The tailors' trick was working.

14

Follow your finger
Run your finger under
the text as you read.
Your child will soon begin to
follow the words with you.

Look at the pictures

Talk about the pictures. They will help your child to understand the story.

"Make me some new clothes." 15

Have a go

Let your child have a go at reading the large type on each right-hand page. It repeats a line from the story.

Join in

When your child is ready, encourage them to join in with the main story text. Shared reading is the first step to reading alone.

Once upon a time there was a foolish emperor.
He loved clothes and had rooms full of clothes.
But the emperor wanted some new clothes.

The emperor wanted some
new clothes.

One day two tailors came to town.
They knew the emperor was foolish.
They wanted to trick the emperor.
"We have some special cloth," they said.
"It is so special that foolish people
cannot see it."

Two tailors came to town.

"Look at the beautiful cloth," they said.
The tailors did not have any cloth.
The emperor could not see the cloth.
But he did not want to look foolish.
"I like the beautiful cloth," he said.

The emperor could not see
the cloth.

"The cloth will make beautiful clothes," said the tailors.
The emperor loved clothes.
He had rooms full of clothes.
"Make me some new clothes," he said.
The tailors' trick was working.

"Make me some new clothes."

The tailors wanted some money.
"We need some money," they said.
"Then we can make you some beautiful clothes."
The emperor gave them some money.
"Come and see the clothes next week," said the tailors.

The emperor gave them
some money.

The next week the emperor went to see
the clothes.
"Look!" said the tailors. "We are
making beautiful clothes."
But the tailors did not have any clothes.
The emperor could not see the clothes.
But he did not want to look foolish.
"I like the beautiful clothes," he said.

The emperor could not see
the clothes.

The tailors wanted some more money.
"We need some more money," they said.
"Then your new clothes will be the best
in the world."
So the emperor gave them some more
money.
The tailors' trick was working.

The emperor gave them some
more money.

The next week the tailors went to see
the emperor.
"Your new clothes are the best in the
world," they said.
The tailors did not have any clothes.
The emperor could not see
the new clothes.
But he did not want
to look foolish.
"My new clothes
are the best in the
world," he said.

The emperor could not see the
new clothes.

The emperor went into town.
"Look at my new clothes," he said.
"They are the best in the world."

The people could not see the clothes.
But they did not want to look foolish.
"Look at the emperor's new clothes,"
they said.

The emperor went into town.

A boy and a girl saw the emperor.
They could not see the new clothes.
They could see the tailors' trick.
The boy said to the girl, "The emperor
has no clothes on."
Then everyone laughed…
at themselves, the tailors
and the foolish emperor.

"The emperor has no clothes on."

Look back in your book.

Can you read these words?

emperor

tailors

girl   boy

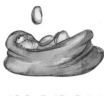

money

clothes

Can you answer these questions?

What did the emperor love most?

Who offered to make the emperor new clothes?

Who said, "The Emperor has no clothes on." ?

First Readers

(subject to availability)

Beauty and the Beast
Chicken Licken
Cinderella
The Elves and the Shoemaker
The Emperor's New Clothes
The Enormous Turnip
The Gingerbread Man
Goldilocks and the Three Bears
Hansel and Gretel
Jack and the Beanstalk
Little Red Riding Hood
The Princess and the Pea
Rapunzel
Rumpelstiltskin
Sleeping Beauty
Snow White and the Seven Dwarfs
The Three Billy Goats Gruff
The Three Little Pigs
The Ugly Duckling